With Feathers and Feelings

By Jared Goodykoontz

D1401016

LABC Book #3

Dedicated to
My God
My Wife
My Daughter
My Family
My Friends
& My LDBB Family

15% of the profits from this book go to the Ohio Ornithological Society
For more info on all their great work: www.ohiobirds.org

Jared Goodykoontz loves connecting with all life around him: human, furred, feathered, scaled, slimy, leafy. He is so grateful that he gets to explore and learn with lots of kiddos every week on indoor/outdoor adventures in Columbus, Ohio. He also loves this painting of an Indigo Bunting he and his 2 year-old daughter Annelise did together!

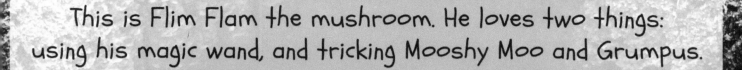
This is Flim Flam the mushroom. He loves two things: using his magic wand, and tricking Mooshy Moo and Grumpus.

He also really enjoys monologues.

Meanwhile at Grumpus' Magic Spot...

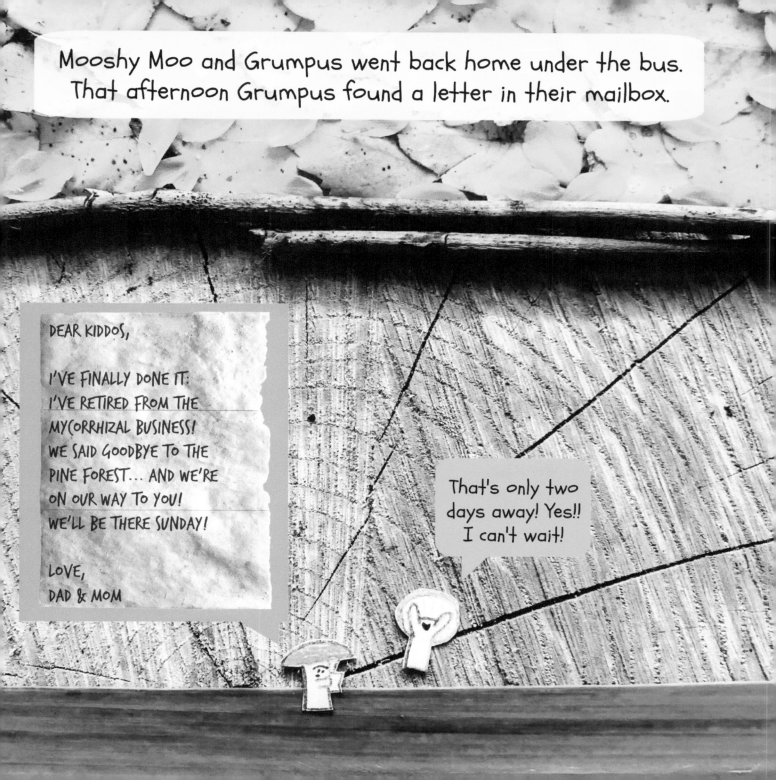

Mooshy Moo and Grumpus went back home under the bus.
That afternoon Grumpus found a letter in their mailbox.

NOW what are we gonna do?! Mom and Dad will be here in 2 days!

We need magic to fix this... hmmm

Well the only magic I know of around here is Flim Flam's... obviously HE isn't going to help!

Wait... I've got it! I know how we can fix this!!

How?

We will use our new wings to fly and find Flim Flam and he will turn us back!

What?! No! I literally just said we can't do that.

We'll figure it out. Let's go find Flim Flam!

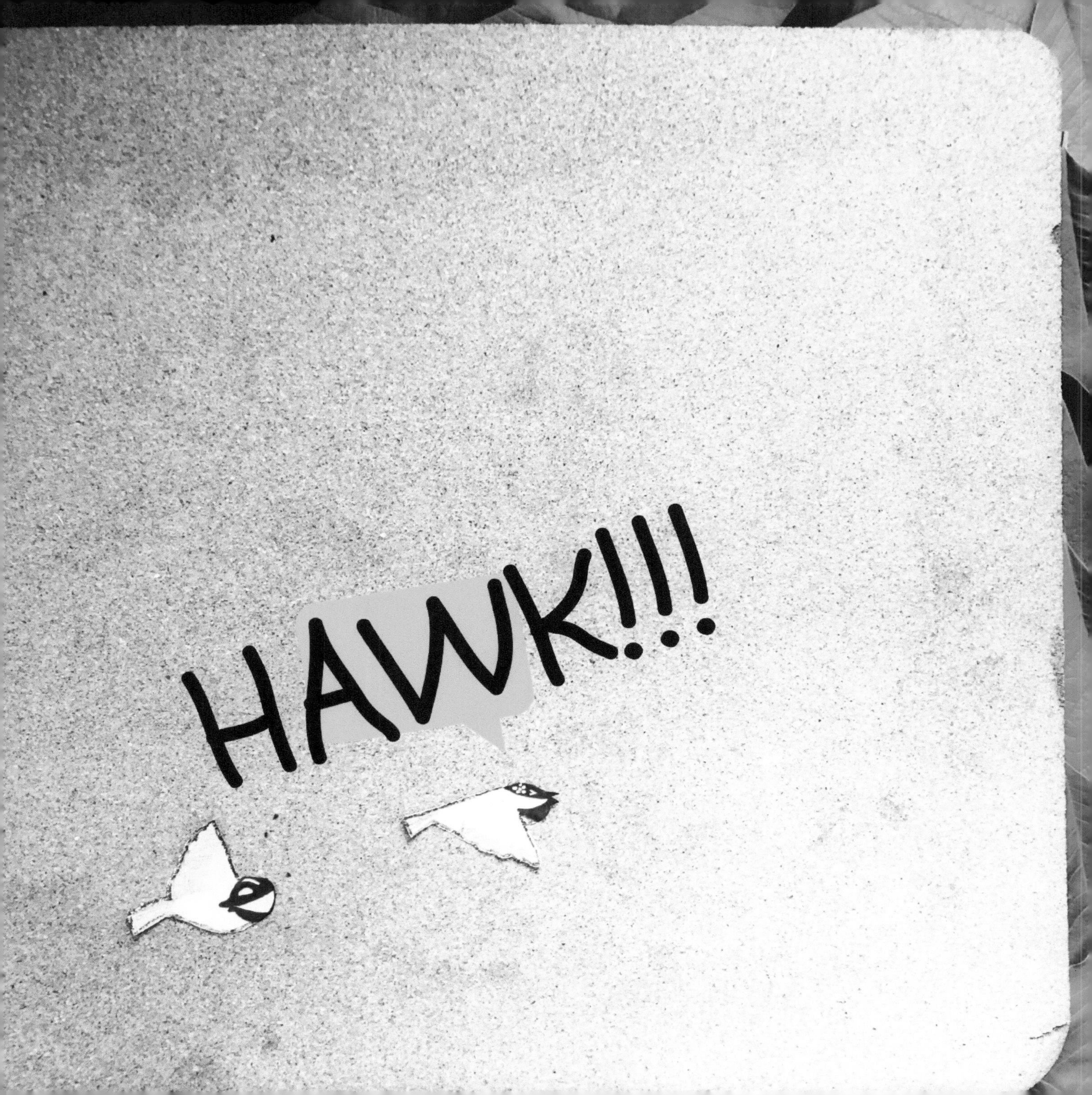
HAWK!!!

The Cooper's Hawk just missed the siblings as they dove into a nearby Oak tree. They soon realized they were not alone.

Didn't you guys hear our alarm calls?! Were you two born yesterday or what?

Well... sort of.

A tricky purple mushroom wizard with a mustache turned us into Chickadees... we're actually mushrooms. I'm Mooshy Moo and this is my brother Grumpus.

The irritated Chickadee introduced himself as Dart and agreed to help these odd birds. They followed him to his nearby flock.

Dumplin had found a feeder. The flock explained some language basics as they ate.

A cat! Mooshy Moo and Grumpus watched as their flock and other birds teamed up to yell at the predator.

Grumpus looked to the sky and...

The morning of their parents' arrival, Mooshy Moo and Grumpus were rudely awakened... again.

CHICK-A-DEE-DEE-DEE

DEE-DEE-DEE-DEE-DEE!!!

In the light of the morning, Dart found Flim Flam.
Grumpus joined the forming mob as the tricky wizard prepared a spell.

"Do you want to come to our party?" Mooshy Moo asked.
Grumpus was shocked, "Wait, WHAT?!"
Flim Flam stopped mid-spell.

Flim Flam and the flock headed over to the bus. Everyone helped get the bus party-ready... even the powerful purple wizard himself!

wha-wha-wha!

MOM & DAD YAY!

Mirdseed, Lirdseed, Fill my hat with...

chip!

chip!

burp!

gurgle

After turning the siblings back into mushrooms, Flim Flam put on a magic show for their feathered friends. Dart and Fee Bee flew off to begin nest scouting while Dumplin "helped" with the cake.

Extension Ideas
Try these out on your own and with your family and friends!

Be a Chickadee

What if YOU got turned into a Chickadee?
You can pretend to be a Chickadee in your yard, your neighborhood or a park. It's even more fun as a flock!

First, look around for a high up hole in a tree to roost in

Then search plants/trees/the air for bugs and berries to eat (but don't eat anything for real!)

You can pretend you have a nest in the roost and have to keep bringing your chicks bugs to eat. After feeding you can sing "Fee Bee! Fee Bay!" to let everyone know your spot is taken.

Remember these language tips:
-say "peep" like Marco Polo to stay in touch with your flock

-sing "Fee Bee! Fee Bay!" to claim territory and express happiness!

-say "Chick-a-dee-dee-dee!" if you find food or a predator like a woodpecker, perched hawk/owl, or a cat (more scary=more "dees")

-say "SEEEEEEEEEE!" and hide if you see a flying hawk

Checkout these awesome bird & bird language websites:
www.allaboutbirds.org
www.animaldiversity.org
www.birdlanguage.com
www.nature-mentor.com
jimmccormac.blogspot.com

...and these super awesome bird books!:
What the Robin Knows by Jon Young
Hawk Rising by Maria Gianferrari
Squawk!

Baby Bongo
the Seagull
by Brynn T.

How do birds make you feel?
I asked people of all ages and this is what they had to say:

"Hearing their song soothes my soul."
~Mindy P. Sykes

"Birds lift my spirits!"
~James Holsinger

"They are amazing creatures that always make me smile."
~Tara Hutson

"Birds make me feel hopeful and strong; like I know a secret, because I know their names and their songs."
~Tara Nicodemus

"A sense of wonder... where have they been, where are they going?"
~Jeannine Julian

"I go out birding and become calm and tranquil and very close to God."
~Renee Frederick

"...freedom."
~Harold Fisher

Checkout Mooshy Moo & Grumpus' other nature connection adventure books:

Where the Adventure is (Five Senses)
&
Right Where You Are (Tracking Animals)
& more coming soon!

Here are some cool Robin tracks from Rohan's porch he wanted everyone to see!

To get these and find more naturey goodness, go to:
www.facebook.com/jgoodstories

CPSIA information can be obtained
at www.ICGtesting.com
Printed in the USA
LVHW072303150421
684658LV00002B/11